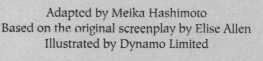

Adapted by Meika Hashimoto
Based on the original screenplay by Elise Allen
Illustrated by Dynamo Limited

Special thanks to Vicki Jaeger, Monica Okazaki, Kathleen Warner, Emily Kelly, Sarah Quesenberry,
Carla Alford, Julia Phelps, Tanya Mann, Rob Hudnut, Shelley Dvi-Vardhana, Michelle Cogan,
Greg Winters, Taia Morley, and Dynamo Limited

A GOLDEN BOOK • NEW YORK

Published in the United States by Golden Books, an imprint of Random House Children's Books, a division of Random House,
Inc., 1745 Broadway, New York, NY 10019, and in Canada by Random House of Canada Limited, Toronto. No part of this book
may be reproduced or copied in any form without permission from the copyright owner. Golden Books, A Golden Book,
A Little Golden Book, the G colophon, and the distinctive gold spine are registered trademarks of Random House, Inc.
www.randomhouse.com/kids
Educators and librarians, for a variety of teaching tools, visit us at www.randomhouse.com/teachers
Library of Congress Control Number: 2010920729
ISBN: 978-0-375-86164-2
Printed in the United States of America
10 9 8 7 6 5 4 3 2

Barbie couldn't wait to visit her aunt Millicent in Paris! Her aunt owned a fashion house called Millicent's. It was always full of fabulous ideas, creative energy, and beautiful dresses.

Barbie brought her pet poodle, Sequin, along for the trip. As the plane began to descend, Barbie could hardly contain her excitement. She hoped her time in the city would be full of adventure—and, of course, fashion!

But when Barbie arrived at Millicent's, she found the
fashion house dark and quiet. Boxes and empty clothing
racks filled the showroom. Not a dress was in sight.

"Barbie! It's good to see you!" Millicent said as she
hugged her niece. She introduced Barbie to her
assistant, Alice, an aspiring designer.

Alice told Barbie that a mean designer named
Jacqueline had stolen all of Millicent's designs. With
no outfits to sell, Millicent had begun to lose money—
and her confidence. A short time later, she closed
her shop.

Millicent was heartbroken. She had decided to sell the building to a company called Hotdogeteria.

Barbie understood just how her aunt felt. Barbie had been fired from her last movie because she didn't agree with the director. Now she was having doubts about how good an actress she was.

"This place . . . I just remember it being so alive and . . . magical!" Barbie said.

Suddenly, Alice had an idea. She quickly led Barbie to an old wardrobe in the attic.

"The very first fashion house in Paris was right here in this building," Alice explained. "It is said that magical creatures appeared from inside an ancient wardrobe to help famous designers."

Desperate to learn the magic of the wardrobe, Barbie and Alice investigated. They soon discovered a poem hidden in one of the attic walls.

Alice put a dress that she had designed into the wardrobe. Then she and Barbie read the poem aloud. All of a sudden, colorful sparkles lit up within the wardrobe. Out came three beautiful Flairies—Glimmer, Shimmer, and Shyne! The Flairies had glitterized Alice's dress into a sparkling masterpiece.

"Our magic only works on designs that we love," the Flairies said. Barbie and Alice were amazed!

Suddenly, a customer came into the store and saw the newly glitterized gown.

"I must have that dress!" the lady gushed.

That gave Barbie an idea. If Alice could design an entire fashion line with the Flairies, then Millicent could hold a fashion show and raise enough money to save her fashion house!

Barbie and Alice worked for hours and hours to create many dazzling dresses. The Flairies added glitter and shine to all the beautiful clothes. "We'll get lots of people to come to the fashion show! They're sure to buy our designs," Barbie said to Alice.

Meanwhile, Jacqueline and her assistant, Delphine, had been spying on Millicent's. They saw how the Flairies were helping Barbie and Alice. "I have to make them mine!" Jacqueline declared. The two designers soon Flairy-napped Glimmer, Shimmer, and Shyne!

Jacqueline ordered the Flairies to glitterize her dresses.

"Our magic doesn't last long on designs that we don't love," they warned her, but Jacqueline wouldn't listen. She made the Flairies turn her ugly clothes into glittering gowns.

Jacqueline decided to hold her own fashion show—on the same night as Millicent's show!

Back at Millicent's, Barbie's aunt was amazed by all of Alice and Barbie's designs. "You're brave enough to follow your passion, no matter what people might say. That's true style!"

Inspired by Alice's belief in herself, Millicent helped the girls finish making the dresses. Barbie couldn't wait for the fashion show—but where were the Flairies?

Later that night, Barbie's poodle, Sequin, and
Millicent's cat and dog, Jilliana and Jacques, noticed
sparkling lights in the window of Jacqueline's shop.
The lights were coming from the Flairies! The trapped
Flairies had lit up the store window, hoping to get the
pets' attention. The three furry friends rushed off to
rescue Glimmer, Shimmer, and Shyne.

Meanwhile, Millicent's fashion show was about to begin. Alice was nervous about how the crowd would like her fashions. And Barbie was nervous about modeling the new designs. But the two friends reminded each other that if they believed in themselves, everything would work out just fine.

At Jaqueline's fashion show, the models walked
down the runway. Suddenly, all of Jacqueline's dresses
transformed into trash! The Flairies' magic had worn off.
"No!" cried Jacqueline. "This can't be happening!"
Horrified, the crowd hurried out. But the people
noticed sparkling lights coming from Millicent's and
crossed the street to see what was going on.

Barbie looked out at the growing crowd at Millicent's and took a deep breath before starting the show.

Dress after glittering dress, the crowd burst into applause. As Barbie walked down the runway in the last gown, the Flairies gave the dress a little extra glimmer, shimmer, and shine.

The crowd loved all the fashions—and thought
Barbie was an amazing model!

After the show, everyone placed orders for the
beautiful dresses. Millicent would have enough
money to save her fashion house!

"We did it!" Barbie said to Alice and Millicent. "We believed in ourselves, and the audience loved us!"

"Magic happens when you believe in yourself," said Alice, and they watched the Flairies sparkle away into the night.